D0031696

REVENGE OF
ZOMBERT

REVENGE OF ZOMBERT

Kara LaReau

illustrated by Ryan Andrews

CANDLEWICK PRESS

Text copyright © 2022 by Kara LaReau
Illustrations copyright © 2022 by Ryan Andrews

First edition 2022

Library of Congress Catalog Card Number 2021948370
ISBN 978-1-5362-0108-6

22 23 24 25 26 27 LBM 10 9 8 7 6 5 4 3 2 1

Printed in Melrose Park, IL, USA

This book was typeset in ITC Mendoza Roman.
The illustrations were created digitally.

Candlewick Press
99 Dover Street
Somerville, Massachusetts 02144

www.candlewick.com

A JUNIOR LIBRARY GUILD SELECTION

For all those who refuse to follow the horde
KL

For Snowy
RA

CHAPTER ONE

He remembered the last night he saw his brother.

Had it been months? A year? Longer? Time was hard to measure in the Cold Place, far from the woods where he and Brother and Sister were born, where their mother had cared for them before she'd disappeared. Then the Rough Hands had come to the woods, and captured them, and brought them all here. And started their experiments.

On that last night, he and Brother were both so weak, from whatever the Rough Hands had given them. But Brother was weaker. He moaned in the adjoining cage.

"It's all right," he'd said to Brother. "I'm here."

"I'm so tired," Brother replied, his voice barely a whisper.

"I know. Stay with me," he'd said. "Stay with me."

"You're the strong one," Brother had said. "Always have been. Sister knew it, too."

Sister. She'd been the smallest of their litter, and the loudest. She'd been in the cage on his other side, until she'd grown weak, too. And then she was quiet forever. The Rough Hands had come in the night and taken her away.

"Stay with me," he'd said again. And again. And again.

But then the Rough Hands came and took Brother away, too.

"You're alive," he said now.

"You sound surprised," Brother replied. His voice was low now, and growling. His body was big, his back muscular, his thick tail twitching aggressively. And his eyes were cold.

"When the Rough Hands took you away, you never returned. Like Sister. I feared the worst."

"Sister was weak. I am strong," Brother said. He narrowed his eyes. "Stronger than you."

CHAPTER TWO

I don't understand," Greg said.

Kari barely understood what was going on, either, but Greg was even further behind, as usual. Why did he always expect her to explain everything to him? He followed her off of the elevator to the lab, where she punched in the key code.

"The Big Boss decided to introduce the Yummconium formula to the people of Lambert,"

Kari said. "It was in the free food at the Harvest Festival."

"I didn't realize the Yummconium formula was ready," Greg said.

Kari didn't, either. She didn't want to admit that the Big Boss's decision had been a surprise. But it seemed obvious now why the Big Boss had been so adamant that the food at the festival be free. They were supposed to be giving something "special" to Lambert that day. Kari had no idea how special. But she couldn't admit this to Greg. He was supposed to be the clueless one.

"If the Big Boss thought it was ready, it must be," Kari said.

"But, I mean . . . is it legal to give it to people without them knowing?" Greg asked. "That seems wrong."

"That's for the Big Boss to worry about. We need to check on the research subjects," Kari said. She strode into the lab and grabbed her YummPad.

"I guess," said Greg. "Though it seems like everyone in Lambert is a research subject now. Except for us, of course."

"Mroooooow," said the cat in cage Y-91. It sat very still and regarded them both with wide yellow eyes.

"We can't let this one get away again," said Kari, leaning in. "This cat is the only animal still living with the original formula. We thought it killed him, but it looks like that formula created all the effects we were hoping for: the heightened senses, the increased brain function, the regenerative powers, and the increased appetite."

"And this one?" Greg asked, pointing at the cat in cage Y-92.

"We thought Y-92 hadn't reacted well to the original formula, either, so we gave it the new formula, the one we're now calling Yummconium," Kari said, tapping through results on her YummPad. "It has all the effects of the original, with two additions: weakened inhibitions and violent tendencies. You don't want to get in between this one and whatever it's craving."

"So . . . that's what everyone in Lambert was given?" Greg asked.

At that moment, Y-92 growled and Kari and Greg jumped back. It bared its fangs and batted at the bars of its cage.

What have we started? Kari thought.

CHAPTER THREE

"I t looks like just about everyone in town is here," Danny said when we finally got to Super YummCo.

I blinked, taking it all in. "And they're consuming everything in sight."

YummCo brings the fun-co!

The fun has just begun-co!

Be smart, not dumb-dumb-dumb-co!

And fill your day with YummCo!

A speaker system on the roof of the Super YummCo Superstore building blared the YummCo jingle over and over and over again. We all covered our ears, but we could still hear it.

"I wish I had earplugs," Carl Weems said.

"Are *you* gonna go in there and buy some?" asked Owen Brown.

"Probably . . . not," said Carl.

The people of Lambert had turned into zombies. Their eyes were glassy and many of them were drooling. They were all pushing and shoving and scrambling over one another to get through the front doors of the store. Eventually, a few people tore the doors off altogether.

"Whoa," I said.

"Zombies don't usually have superstrength," said Danny. He was a horror movie buff, so he was an expert.

"Maybe they just want what's inside that much," said Nina.

Several people fell in the stampede, but the others just stepped over them, or even on them. I couldn't

bear to watch, even though I knew I had to, as one of the few witnesses. My mother and father were somewhere in that horde, along with everyone else's parents. When I returned to our house earlier that day after the Harvest Festival, my dad was gorging himself on ice cream and my mom was gorging her credit card on the YummCo website. It was like a nightmare; even now, thinking about it made me feel nauseous. Really nauseous, like I wanted to pass out or throw up, or both.

"Why are they zombies and we're not?" Owen asked.

"It can't be because we're kids," Nina said. "I see just about everyone from school in there."

She was right. Todd Kaplan and Chelsea DiSanto and Logan Sands had already come out of the store and were crouched over bags of candy and a case of YummPop in the parking lot. Their faces and hands were sticky as they tried to push each other out of the way of the sweets. Their parents were right behind them with grocery bags. Some were bulging with junk food, others with clothes and makeup, toys, books, and electronics.

"Dad?" Carl said as Mr. Weems emerged from the store on a ride-on lawnmower loaded up with mulch and leaf bags. Mrs. Weems was right behind him, pushing a shopping cart spilling over with crafting supplies.

I yawned.

"Are you . . . bored?" asked Owen. I shook my head.

"She seems tired," said Danny, looking at me. "And pale."

"It's been a long day," I reminded him. "I thought Bert and I were just going to the Lambert Harvest Festival to compete in the Best Pet Contest, and hopefully win. I didn't expect him to be kidnapped by the Yumm family and then find out we're in the middle of a *zombie outbreak.*"

I didn't want to tell him that my body felt prickly all over, like when your arm falls asleep. What was happening to me?

"Should we call the police? They'll know what to do," Owen suggested.

"My phone's not working," Danny said, tapping at its screen. Earlier we'd discovered that video he'd recorded of the Yumms kidnapping Bert had been wiped from his YummPhone.

"YummCo's probably controlling that, too," Owen said.

"Besides, the police are already here. Like that matters," said Carl, motioning to several officers with glassy eyes. They'd tipped over a YummCo Wiener food truck and were jamming hot dogs into their mouths.

"So, what should we do?" Nina asked.

I turned to her to answer, but her face seemed fuzzy, like I was looking through a camera out of focus. I squinted.

"Head back to my house," I managed.

And then everything went black.

CHAPTER FOUR

W ell," the Big Boss said, feet up on the carved mahogany desk. "I'm sure you two have found today . . . interesting."

"Understatement of the year," muttered Greg.

"I just wish we knew about the plan before it was executed," Kari said. "I'm feeling pretty out of the loop here."

"You know about it now," said the Big Boss. "You'll know what you need to know when you need to know it."

"I've been watching on the live feed," Kari noted, glancing down at her YummPad. "It looks like the entire town has arrived at the Super YummCo Superstore. What do we do now?"

"They'll buy anything and everything in the store, and then they'll go home and keep buying online until their credit cards hit their limit. And then we'll give them our new YummCredit cards," the Big Boss said. "We'll give them more and more and more."

"What about the superstore workers?" Greg asked. "And the workers in the factory? How is it that they're still doing their jobs amid all of this?"

The Big Boss chuckled. "It's a little trick called *mesmerism*."

"Mesmer . . . what?" Greg said.

"It means hypnotism," said Kari. She looked at the Big Boss. "You've hypnotized everyone?"

The Big Boss smiled. "Every person who's eaten food containing Yummconium."

"Of course. The Yummconium weakens their inhibitions. Anyone who ingests it will be highly vulnerable to suggestion," Kari said. Her eyes widened. She wasn't sure whether to be impressed or horrified, maybe a little bit of both.

"They'll do anything for us, as long as we keep playing the YummCo jingle over the sound system," the Big Boss continued. "And as long as we keep feeding them Yummconium. The entire town is now under my control. The humans, anyway. It's a shame, really, that animals aren't so similarly suggestible . . ."

"So that's the big plan? Turn everyone in Lambert into zombies so we can profit off of their hunger?" Greg asked.

Kari gave him a nudge.

"What?" Greg asked. "I'm just trying to understand. So I can, you know, be helpful."

"I'm glad you're ready to help, Gregory. If not, we can certainly consider some . . . alternatives," the Big Boss said, opening a desk drawer and revealing two energy bars.

Greg gulped.

YUMMCO POWERYUMM BARS the wrappers said. NOW WITH <u>YUMMCONIUM!</u>

■ ■ ■

As Kari and Greg returned to the lab, they were both shaken. Greg was the only one not trying to hide it.

"I didn't sign on for this, Kari," he said. "Tainted food? Mesmerism? Turning people into zombies against their will?"

"Our employees signed away most of their rights when they took the job; they knew the risks," Kari said.

"Did they, though?" said Greg.

Kari rolled her eyes. "And it's not like the towns-people are doing anything they wouldn't already be doing," she continued. "We're just tapping into their truest impulses."

"Well, not everyone wants their impulses . . . tapped," Greg noted.

"It's the same thing we do with commercials. And with mining people's data, and all our shopping algorithms. We're already able to tell what you want before you want it. We're already able to affect the choices consumers make every day."

"It's not the same thing, and you know it," Greg said.

Deep down, she knew it wasn't the same thing. But if she allowed herself to think that way for too long, everything she's believed and worked toward during her time at YummCo would be one big horrible lie. Kari couldn't let her mind go there. She wouldn't.

"If you don't like it, Greg, you can always consider the 'alternatives' the Big Boss offered you. Or you can try to leave like Walter, who had the job before you did," she said. "He stole files from the lab and ended up having a heart attack from the stress."

"I'll stay," Greg said. "But not because I'm afraid. Because someone has to be the voice of reason here."

Kari scoffed. "Reason" and "Greg" didn't belong in the same sentence.

CHAPTER FIVE

After the Rough Hands returned to the lab, he listened in on their conversation. Finally, he understood their names: Kari and Greg.

And he saw something in their eyes he hadn't seen before. Fear.

"Can you understand them as I do?" he whispered.

"All too well," said Brother.

"These two Rough Hands are afraid," he said. "Too afraid to stop what's happening."

Brother shifted in his cage. "I was afraid once. And so were you, and Sister, and all the others here. The Rough Hands showed us no mercy."

"They're not all like that," he said. "I've known others outside who are kind. Who have cared for me. Who gave me my name: Bert."

"'Bert'?" Brother scoffed, shifting in his cage again. "You're a fool to trust them. The Rough Hands bring nothing but pain. They'll get what they deserve."

"Not if I can help it," Bert said.

"I'm hungry!" Brother growled. "Now! Now! Now!"

"Okay, okay, big fella," said the one called Greg. He turned to the other cages. "Hmm . . . what's on the menu for tonight?"

"Just make sure it's alive, and bigger than those lab mice you gave us earlier," Brother growled. "One way or another, this *hunger . . . must be . . . satisfied!*"

CHAPTER SIX

Bert and I are running through the woods together. I have no trouble keeping up with him as we slip through branches and jump over logs. The wind is in my hair, and the sun is on my face. I can smell the wet autumn leaves, feel the muddy earth beneath my feet, but only barely. I'm running so fast, they hardly touch the ground.

When we get to the river, we stop to rest, but not for long. I open my eyes and Bert has a headless rat in his jaws. He places it at my feet. I've never wanted to eat a rat before, but I'm just so hungry, I can't help myself. I pick it up by the tail, raise it high over my open mouth, and—

■ ■ ■

"Aaaaah!" I screamed, sitting straight up.

"Hey, everyone, she's awake!" Danny announced. He was sitting on my bed, looking at me with wide eyes. "Are you okay?"

The morning sun was streaming through my bedroom window. I shielded my eyes.

"What happened?" I asked.

"You fainted while we were at the Super YummCo Superstore," he explained.

"You had us really worried," Nina said. She was standing in the doorway with Owen and Carl.

"You all . . . slept over?" I asked, sitting up.

Everyone nodded.

"It's not like we have anyone at home waiting for us," Owen reminded me.

"We all took shifts sitting with you to make sure you were okay," Danny said.

I rubbed my eyes. For the longest time, Danny had been my only friend. It felt weird to know other people actually cared about me. Weird in a good way.

"You were talking in your sleep," Owen informed me. "You were saying 'Bert' a lot."

"We're, you know, glad you're not dead," Carl said.

"Oh, thank goodness," Mrs. Witt said, appearing behind them. She came in and sat on the bed next to me and felt my forehead. "It's good you feel normal now. I've been trying to keep you warm since we carried you up here earlier. You were as cold as ice!"

"I must be coming down with whatever the twins had," I said. "Emmett and Ezra are just getting over that cold."

"So, you're not turning into a zombie?" Carl asked.

"Um, no," I said.

"She's not drooling and blank-eyed," Owen noted.

I threw off all the sheets and blankets and slowly stood up.

"Though she does look . . . really pale," Danny said to the others.

"I'm fine."

But I wasn't fine. I felt weak, like I could pass out at any moment. My brain felt fuzzy. And I had a terrible feeling in the pit of my stomach, like it was painfully empty. I managed to push past everyone and stumble down the hallway.

"Is she going to barf?" Carl asked. "Because that would be kind of awesome."

"Shut up," said Nina.

I used what remaining strength I had to make my way downstairs into the kitchen, where I opened the refrigerator. And there it was. My dad's leftover lasagna. I grabbed a fork, took the pan out of the refrigerator, and tore off the aluminum foil. When the smell of the tangy tomatoes and the thick cheese and the garlic and the basil filled my nostrils, I groaned.

"Did you . . . want some of that heated up?" someone asked behind me. But I didn't want to waste a moment to respond. I was too busy cramming forkfuls of lasagna into my mouth.

I can't really explain the flavor; it was as if I could smell and taste every single molecule of every bite, and every time I swallowed, I felt happier than I've ever felt in my life. It was so good, I couldn't stop eating, forkful after forkful, until the entire lasagna was gone. I even licked the pan.

"Whoa," said Owen.

"My mom says, 'Feed a cold, starve a fever,'" Nina said. "And Mellie definitely doesn't have a fever."

I looked down and saw the place on my arm where Bert had scratched me while we were attempting our performance the day before at the Harvest Festival's Best Pet Contest. But there wasn't a scratch on my arm anymore. It had already healed into a thin scar.

All of a sudden, every sound and sensation seemed to intensify. I could feel all my clothes brushing against my skin and the rug tickling my bare feet. I could hear Carl scratching his head, and Owen shifting from one foot to the other, and Nina swallowing. I could hear everyone's heartbeats, including my own. If I really concentrated, I could hear Emmett and Ezra upstairs in their room playing with their train set. And my head felt like it was buzzing. Thoughts and ideas were forming and connecting so fast, I almost couldn't keep up with them.

"Honey, is something wrong?" Mrs. Witt asked.

I wanted to tell them about the scratch and the scar, and the heightened senses, and the buzzy feeling in my head. I wanted to tell them about the dream I'd had earlier, and the fuzzy brain, and the hunger, and the exhaustion that turned into the ultimate happiness when I ate. But if I did, I knew they'd be afraid. And we had work to do.

I let out a long, deep burp.

The answer was clear.

"Everything's great," I said. I reached into the pocket of the lab coat Mrs. Witt had given me, the one that used to be Mr. Witt's when he was still alive. I took out the slip of paper I'd found there and reread the words.

Open the gift that keeps on giving.

"Can we have the key to Mr. Witt's workshop?" I asked Mrs. Witt. "We need to go there. Now."

CHAPTER SEVEN

THE GIFT THAT KEEPS ON GIVING

The workshop was in a shed behind Mrs. Witt's house.

"You said there'd been a break-in here," Danny said. "Did they take anything?"

"No, Mrs. Witt said it looked like someone had rummaged through everything," I replied as I turned the key Mrs. Witt gave me and pulled off the padlock. "There were a few broken test tubes, but maybe that's because they were in a hurry. She figured they were looking for something valuable. Though they didn't take Mr. Witt's microscope; it's worth hundreds of dollars."

Inside, everything was just as Mrs. Witt and I had left it after all our cleaning and organizing. Boxes of lab equipment packed up and ready to be donated to YummCo High School. Floors swept and mopped. Tabletops scrubbed with industrial cleaner. A huge case of YummCo Nutty Clusters, which had been Mr. Witt's favorite snack while he was working. And, in one corner, a few framed pictures in bubble wrap.

"Ugh," I said, holding my nose.

"What?" Danny said.

"The cleaner Mrs. Witt and I used," I said. "That bleachy smell is so strong."

Danny sniffed the air. "Really? I can barely smell it," he said.

I walked over to the pictures and flipped through them until I found the big framed photo of Mr. and Mrs. Witt in front of the Witts Confectionery factory on the day of its grand opening.

"Is that . . . Mr. and Mrs. Witt?" Owen asked. I nodded.

"'Witts Confectionery,'" Nina repeated. "I think my grandma has some of that candy in a bowl at her house. She's always offering it to me, but I thought it looked funny. I mean, it looks old-fashioned, not like the candy you get from YummCo."

"It's not like the candy from YummCo. It's *better*," Danny said.

"Mrs. Witt hands that stuff out at Halloween," Carl added. "It's always my favorite."

"Well, hopefully we're about to find something sweeter here," I said, inspecting the front and back of the frame. Nothing about it looked weird.

"What are you looking for?" Danny asked.

"A place where you could hide something," I said. Carefully, I popped out the thick cardboard backing. All that was behind it was the photo itself and the glass.

"Bummer," said Owen.

"This has to be it," I said, putting the cardboard back. I flipped the frame back over and pointed to the brass plaque. "The note said *Open the gift that keeps on giving*. This plaque says . . ."

Again, my brain started buzzing. The answer clicked into place.

"What? What is it?" asked Nina.

"Does anyone have a screwdriver?" I asked.

"What kind of nerd carries a screwdriver with them?" Carl asked.

I looked at Mrs. Witt's keychain. Dangling from it, along with the key for the padlock and her car keys, was a circular piece of what looked like steel. It was cut into weird shapes, almost like a snowflake. The longer I looked at it, the more it made sense.

"This kind of nerd," I said. I pointed at each of the shapes. "Bottle opener, box cutter, wrench, and Phillips and flathead screwdrivers."

"Cool," said Owen.

I used the Phillips head to take off the screws. Then I held my breath as I lifted the plaque.

"Eureka," I said. Behind the plaque, someone—I was guessing Mr. Witt—had cut out a little compartment.

"What's in it?" Danny asked.

I turned to them and opened my palm. Inside was a thumb drive.

"Now we just need someone's computer. And not a YummBook," I said. "From now on, we can't trust anything that comes from YummCo. We saw what they did to our phones. They could be listening to us or watching us, or both," I explained.

"This workshop might even be . . ." Danny said, lowering his voice, *"bugged."*

Quietly, I screwed the plaque back together, then we all left the workshop. When we got to Mrs. Witt's driveway, Carl was the first one who spoke.

"I asked for a YummBook for Christmas," he said. "Good thing Santa didn't come through. My old computer is slow, but it's not made by YummCo."

"Let's go. We have a lot to figure out," I said. Though my brain was already steps ahead.

CHAPTER EIGHT

The Big Boss stepped into the surveillance chamber and switched on the monitors.

Installing cameras on every street corner was part of the YummCo Safety Initiative a few years ago, in coordination with the police department. According to the press release, it was meant to lower traffic violations and all-around crime rates, but really, it was one of the ways the Big Boss kept an eye on everything. And everyone.

YummCo Animal Pals. YummCo Elementary. YummBrew Coffee Shop. Everything in Lambert bore the YummCo name and was under its control. Now everyone in Lambert was, too.

It was a new day, but the townspeople were still at the Super YummCo Superstore, consuming everything in sight. The receipts from the day were astounding, ten times what they'd been on their best Black Friday sales day. But it wasn't enough. Having control of a town like Lambert was small potatoes.

"Go HUGE or go home," the Big Boss said. "It's time for Phase Two."

CHAPTER NINE

Research

So, you like space," Owen said, looking around at all the NASA posters and outer space decor in Carl's room. "A lot."

"You got a problem with that?" Carl said.

Owen shook his head.

"I'm learning everything I can about it now so I can be ready when we colonize Mars," Carl said, turning on his laptop. "It's happening sooner than we think."

When we put the thumb drive into Carl's laptop, it didn't give us all the answers. Instead, it gave us another question.

"Password?" Danny said.

"Ugh," said Carl.

"Mr. Witt really was careful," said Nina.

"Too careful," said Owen. "Though I guess it's a sign that whatever's on this thumb drive is pretty valuable."

"What do we do now?" Danny asked.

I barely had to think about it; the idea came to me almost immediately.

"Let's go back to my house," I said. "There's only one person we know who can crack this code."

Mrs. Witt was sitting on the floor with the twins when we got there.

"Mellie!" Emmett cried. "We're playing Yummopoly Junior, and I'm winning!"

"No, *I'm* winning!" cried Ezra, holding up a fistful of green-and-brown play money.

"I didn't want to turn on the television," Mrs. Witt explained. "I know it sounds silly, but it feels like YummCo is everywhere."

"It doesn't sound silly at all," I said. In fact, it

gave me an idea. I went to the kitchen and opened our junk drawer. After some rummaging, I found my parents' old phones—the ones they had before they upgraded to YummPhones.

"What are you doing?" Carl asked.

"Making sure we have a safe way to communicate," I said. I plugged in the phones to charge them up and enabled Wi-Fi calling.

"I fed the little ones some frozen pizza I found in the freezer. It wasn't the YummCo brand, so it seemed safe," Mrs. Witt said. "I told them your parents were on a last-minute trip."

As soon as she said the word *pizza*, my stomach growled. I licked my lips.

"Is there . . . any more pizza?" I asked.

"In the kitchen," she said.

It was a good thing she made a lot because everyone else was hungry, too. But I was beyond hungry, even though I'd inhaled that lasagna just a few hours before. I was working on my third slice when Mrs. Witt was typing in her first password attempt.

INCORRECT PASSWORD.

"What did you type in?" Danny asked.

"My name," she said. "I was sure that would be it. It's either 'Candy' or our anniversary."

She typed in the date and hit return.

INCORRECT PASSWORD.

"Darn," said Owen. "What happens if we don't get it on the third try?"

"If it's anything like my parents' computer, it means we get locked out," Carl said. "Game over."

"Okay, let's think," I said through a mouthful of pizza. "What else does Mr. Witt like? I bet it was something he saw in his workshop every day, so it was a word he couldn't forget."

"Chemistry?" offered Carl.

"Microscope?" said Nina.

"Maybe one of the elements in the periodic table?" Danny suggested. "Though we'd have to guess which one."

"Test tube? Beaker? Bunsen burner?" said Carl.

"Lab coat or goggles?" said Mrs. Witt. "He wore those every day."

They all seemed possible, but not quite right. I

closed my eyes. My belly felt warm and full of pizza, and that warmth was spreading through my whole body. I felt happy, and powerful, like I could do anything. My mind buzzed with ideas. And then . . .

I laughed. Then I grabbed the laptop.

"*Nuttyclusters*," I said as I typed it in.

"Of course," said Mrs. Witt.

I hit return. The screen flickered, and then it went black.

"Oh, no," Nina moaned.

Then the screen went green . . . and brown.

"Oh, YES! We're in!" Carl said. "Genius!" He high-fived me. Did Carl Weems, my once archnemesis, just call me a genius? I had to admit, it felt good.

"But what's all this?" Danny asked.

I clicked on a folder marked Correspondence. Inside were files of saved emails from Stuart Yumm, with directives and requests for progress reports, all mentioning something called Project Y-C.

"The 'Y-C' must be for 'YummCo,'" Carl said.

I clicked on a folder called Research. The first few files were just articles.

"Articles about bugs? What do *bugs* have to do with anything?" Nina asked.

"This is an article about a parasitic fungus that controls the minds of ants," I said, clicking another file. "And this one is about an organism that releases chemicals into an insect's brain when it's ingested."

"I remember learning about this in school. It's called *neuroparasitology*," Mrs. Witt said. "Neurotoxins can be used by parasites to hijack the decision-making ability of their hosts."

"Sounds a lot like what's been happening to everyone in town," Danny said.

"But worse," Owen noted.

I thought about my parents, how my dad kept eating and my mom kept buying things, and how angry my mom seemed when I tried to get her to stop. They were being controlled by a parasitic host, and that host was YummCo. Were Bert and I being controlled, too? If so, why weren't we mind-controlled zombies like the rest of Lambert?

"I don't understand how Bert fits in to all of this," Danny said. "He definitely has a big appetite, but he's not violent."

"He did lunge at me that one time," Carl reminded him.

"That's because he was protecting Mellie," Danny said. "You were being a jerk."

I raised my eyebrows. He wasn't wrong.

"There's a lot of chemical formulas here," I said. "I recognize the elements, but not how they're working together."

Mrs. Witt leaned in. "It looks like they've synthesized one or more of the neurotoxins and used them in a formula for something called . . . *Yummconium*."

"Did they give everyone Yummconium somehow? And if so, why are we the only ones who aren't affected?" Carl asked.

Speak for yourself, I thought. Though maybe Carl was on to something. I stood up and started pacing, my mind buzzing again.

"We aren't affected," I said. I was the exception, of course, but I knew I'd been infected by Bert.

I turned to Mrs. Witt. "And you and the twins aren't affected. You and the twins didn't go to the Harvest Festival."

"But the rest of us here did," said Nina.

"We did . . . but we didn't eat anything. Even though they had all that free food," Danny said. He pointed to each of us. "Mellie and I didn't eat anything. Carl's mom wouldn't let him eat anything before his performance in the Best Pet Contest . . ."

"I couldn't eat the food because of my allergies," Nina recalled.

"And Mudge wouldn't stop squawking until I went back home and got his cuttlebone, so I didn't have time to eat before the performance," Owen said. "Do you think the Yummconium was in the food?"

I remembered my parents sharing a YummDog after Bert and I performed in the Best Pet Contest. I was so distracted by how weird Bert was acting and how he'd scratched me, and the whole time they were probably eating Yummconium right in front of me.

"It must have been," I said. "Everyone started acting weird right after the parade. That's when the festival ended."

"Then it makes sense that everyone in town went to Super YummCo. That's where all the food is," Danny said.

"And everything else you might have an appetite for," I said.

"What happens when Super YummCo runs out of things to buy?" Owen asked.

We all looked at each other.

"We need to find a way to stop this," I said. "There has to be an antidote to Yummconium."

"Yeah, probably. But it's at YummCo somewhere," Danny said. "I bet it's in the lab where that jerk Greg works."

"And Kari, the one who took Bert away," I added. Thoughts were flashing through my brain so fast, it almost hurt. I remembered how Bert looked at the end of the Harvest Festival as Kari took him from my arms and placed him right in Stuart Yumm's clutches. I hoped he was okay. There was no telling what Stuart

Yumm and his scientists would do to him, so I needed to find a way to get to him first.

"But we'd need to get into the lab. How could we do that without working there?" Nina asked.

"Through the passageway," Mrs. Witt said.

"Passageway?" Danny said.

"When Walter and I bought the original building for the confectionery, we found a passageway underneath; evidently it was used for bootlegging during Prohibition. It leads from the factory up to the mansion."

"They must have had some *serious* parties out there back then," Carl said.

"And that's the mansion where the Yumms live now," said Nina.

Mrs. Witt nodded. "Now it runs between the mansion and the corporate office and research and development lab. You can find a pretty clear layout on the blueprint we had framed. I think it's still in Walt's workshop."

"Do you think the passageway is still open?" Carl asked.

"The Yumms might not even know it's there," Mrs. Witt said. "I don't think we ever mentioned it when we sold the building. They'd really have to scrutinize the blueprints to see it. Though the entrance at the mansion might be more obvious."

"Whether they know about it or not, it's our only way in," I said. "Let's grab the blueprints from Mr. Witt's shed and ride to Yumm Mansion."

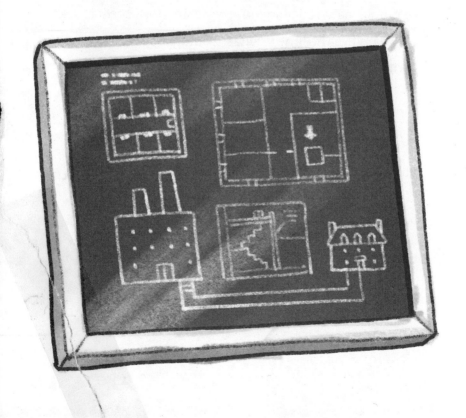

"Wait until those phones are fully charged. I'll take one and you can keep the other," Mrs. Witt said. "I wish I could go with you, but I can't leave the twins here."

"Don't worry, we'll definitely be in touch," I said. "Especially if anything with chemistry is involved."

After a few more minutes, the phones were fully charged. I put one in my backpack, along with a granola bar. If I got hungry again, I wanted to be prepared. Who knew what would happen if I went without food for too long?

CHAPTER TEN

H e'd made short work of the lab mice, even though they lacked the flavor of the field mice he'd caught in the woods. When the hunger was kept at bay, Bert could think.

It was time. He looked around, at the one called Greg eating his lunch, at the one called Kari making notes, at the other cages filled with other animals. Those that weren't sedated looked on sorrowfully.

"Before I escaped, I promised I'd come back for those I left behind," he whispered. "I couldn't save them. But now I'm stronger than I was before. And smarter. I have a plan."

In the adjoining cage, Brother rolled on his side, snoring, his belly bulging with his latest kills. He wasn't as menacing when he slept; he was still enormous, but with his eyes closed, he looked as he had as a kitten, vulnerable and innocent.

"I'm going to rescue you," Bert whispered. "All of you."

CHAPTER ELEVEN

We left our bikes at the front gate. I spoke into the intercom.

"Hello? Mr. Yumm?" I said. "It's Mellie Gore. You took my cat . . . er, I guess it was your cat?"

"Mr. Yumm is very busy at the moment," a voice said, the connection crackling.

"We have video of some *very suspicious behavior* at the festival," I said.

"No, we don't," said Danny.

I nudged him. "They don't know that," I whispered. I turned back to the intercom. "We were hoping we could talk."

The intercom was silent for a few long seconds. Then it crackled.

"Come in," the voice said.

BZZZZZZT!

I covered my ears at the sound. It was so loud, but it didn't seem to bother anyone else. Then the gate opened.

"Well," said Carl. "Here goes nothing."

We made our way up the winding driveway to the mansion. I'd never been there before, past those manicured lawns and topiary sculptures in the shape of the letter Y. Even the fountain was shaped like a Y, spraying green-colored water into the air.

"Impressive," Danny said.

"Really? I think it's a bit . . . much," Nina said.

A huge letter Y was carved into each of the two huge wooden front doors.

"Should we . . . knock?" Owen asked.

"Look—there's a bell," Carl said, pressing it. The

chimes rang out a familiar melody: the YummCo jingle.

"The more I hear that, the creepier it sounds," Danny said. I shivered in agreement.

For a good couple of minutes, we didn't hear anything. Then we heard a click.

I tried the door. "It's open," I said.

"Whoa," said Owen, looking up at the green-and-brown glass chandelier in the entryway.

"You said it," Danny replied. "This entryway is bigger than my whole apartment."

"I can't believe everything is green and brown, even in here," Nina whispered, looking at the color-coordinated drapes and furniture and rugs.

"Do you hear that?" I said.

"No. I don't hear anything," said Carl.

"Shh," said Danny.

Everyone stopped to listen. Faintly, music was piped in through overhead speakers. Though it sounded a lot like classical piano, there was no mistaking the tune.

"It's the YummCo jingle," I whispered. "It's *everywhere.*"

Suddenly we heard heels click-clacking on the hardwood floors, and Yolanda appeared.

"Children," she said, smiling. "Please, follow me."

"Where's Mr. Yumm?" Danny asked. "We came to talk to him."

"He's . . . indisposed right now. We've all been busy, trying to sort out what's happening here in town. It's all so horrifying." She guided us into the living room and swept her hand over the longest sofa I'd ever seen. "Please, sit down. Make yourselves comfortable."

The last thing I wanted to do was get "comfortable," but I reminded myself that we were on a mission. We all sat. Yolanda sat in a chair across from us, crossed her legs, and put her hands in her lap primly.

"I'm so sorry about that . . . episode with the police yesterday afternoon," Yolanda said. "You might have come to see that animal as your pet, but it's actually quite dangerous, and it belongs in our lab, under observation. The last thing I'd want is for any of you children to get hurt. By the way, can I interest you in a snack?"

She swept a hand across the coffee table, where a tray of drinks and a plate of YummCo Fudgeroo cookies were laid out. They smelled amazing; I could detect every note of chocolate and buttery caramel and vanilla. Thankfully I'd eaten a lot of pizza earlier, so I was still full . . . for now.

"I love Fudgeroos," said Owen.

"Absolutely not," said Nina, bumping his hand as he reached out for the cookie plate.

"Right," said Owen. He folded his arms. "No, thank you."

"Now. I'm sure my father will be eager to hear about your video," Yolanda said. "What kind of suspicious behavior did you happen to film?"

"First, can I use your bathroom?" I asked. "I drank a YummPop earlier, and I really need to pee."

"The closest bathroom is down the hall, on the right," she said, motioning in that direction. As I got up, Danny and I locked eyes, and he gave me a little nod. *Here goes nothing,* I thought.

I pulled out the blueprint and studied it as I crept down the hall. It looked like the passageway entrance would be a few doors past the bathroom. But when I opened that door, it led me into what looked like Mr. Yumm's study.

The reddish-brown wooden desk was huge and carved with thorny vines. All around the room were framed photos of Yolanda with different celebrities and politicians, and posters of her book covers, and a huge framed photo of her behind his desk. Mr. Yumm really did love his daughter. And he loved books; there were tall shelves lining the walls, filled mainly with books about business. But one bookcase caught my eye; all the titles on those shelves were about science. Some were about chemistry. Some were about insects. I pulled one of the insect books off the shelf and opened it where someone had left a sticky note. It was a chapter about neuroparasitology.

Next to the insect book was a book called *Mesmerism for the Masses*.

"What is *mesmerism?*" I whispered to myself, flipping through it, my brain buzzing.

"It's another word for hypnosis," a voice said.

I turned around. Yolanda stood in the doorway, her arms folded.

"Sorry, I got lost on the way to the bathroom," I said. "And I just love books."

Danny and the others appeared behind Yolanda in the hallway.

"Your friend here was just telling me about the video he shot at the festival," Yolanda said. "Evidently he saw someone tampering with the food?"

I swallowed. "None of us ate any," I said. "That's why we haven't . . . changed."

"That makes sense," she said. "But you know what doesn't make sense?"

I shook my head.

"How could he have a video when we wiped everyone's YummPhones after the festival ended? And how could he have seen someone tampering with food at the festival when the Yummconium was added at the factory?" she said coolly.

She walked over to the desk and sat down. That's when I noticed that while the desk was huge, the chair behind it was small. Too small for Mr. Yumm.

I looked at the huge photo of Yolanda on the wall behind her and all the other photos of her around the room. All at once, it clicked into place.

I gasped. "You're the one in charge," I said. "Not Mr. Yumm. It's been you all along."

Yolanda laughed. "Of course, you assumed it was all my father. Just like everyone else. *My father* has absolutely no vision. When he finally figured out my plan yesterday, he actually tried to stop me. But I figured out a way to deal with him."

She put her dainty feet up on the desk.

"They call me the Big Boss," she said. She smiled, showing all of her perfect teeth. "I've been underestimated all my life. Daddy never even considered handing the company over to me when he retired; he thought I was just a silly little girl with weird little science hobbies. That's what's allowed me to get ahead, when no one else is looking. I'm sure you can relate—we have a lot in common, Emmeline."

She might have been right about some of that. I did feel overlooked sometimes by my family, and some kids at school like Carl did think I was weird.

But I wasn't selfish or evil like Yolanda. And I wasn't about to let her mesmerize me, though I did want to keep her talking.

"So, Bert was one of your test subjects?" I asked.

"We put the original formula in its food. Y-91 seemed to respond . . . poorly," Yolanda explained. "Now we know it just takes some time to enter the bloodstream. Since Y-91 tore off the ID tag on its ear when it escaped, we had no way to track it. I've been looking for that animal ever since. And trying to find ways to get it back so I can conduct further experiments. Though, thankfully, I've had no shortage of test subjects on which to perfect my formula. The new Yummconium has exceeded all expectations for reducing impulse control and inducing the appetite."

"But it also induces violence," Danny noted.

For a second, Yolanda glared at him. Then her mouth spread into her trademark smile. "A person who can't stop buying your product, who would do *anything* for it?" she said. "That's what I call the perfect consumer."

My brain buzzed with thoughts. So that's why

Bert's ear was bloody when we found him, because he'd wisely removed his tracking tag. And he didn't have any fur because they'd probably shaved him to conduct their experiments.

And then I realized something else. "Remember that team in hazmat suits last month? The one we ran into that night near Super YummCo?" I said to Danny. He nodded. "They were looking for *Bert*!"

Yolanda nodded. "Then we sponsored that special at YummCo Animal Pals, offering free pet exams," she continued. "If you'd just brought Y-91 in, you would have made things a lot less complicated."

"Mellie did try to bring Bert in," Danny said. He was right; I had tried to take Bert for a checkup at YummCo Animal Pals.

"But he freaked out and ran away," I added. "Now I know why—you and Mr. Yumm were there, and Bert was afraid of *you*."

"Well, when those plans didn't work, I came up with the plan for the Best Pet Contest. And that led me to consider testing my improved Yummconium formula on an even wider pool of test subjects,"

Yolanda said, examining her manicure. "So I suppose I actually have *you* to thank, Mellie Gore."

Yolanda pressed a button underneath her desk, and the wall panel behind her where her full-length photo hung swung open. Three huge YummCo workers strode into the study, all with glassy eyes. So that's where the secret passageway was; I'd been standing near it the whole time.

"Take these children to the lab and lock them up," Yolanda instructed them. "When you return, I'll have a feast waiting for you."

"Run!" Danny shouted. Even though we had no idea where we were going, we rushed past the three zombie workers and down the hallway. Instead of taking a right into the living room, we took a left and ended up in the dining room, where a familiar figure sat at the head of the long table, his back to us.

"Mr. Yumm?" Carl said.

"Maybe he can actually help us," Owen whispered.

"Remember us, sir, from the Best Pet Contest at the Harvest Festival? I was the one with the amazing rats, who really deserved to win," Carl said, stepping toward him. "Now your daughter has turned the whole town into zombies. We need your help!"

As we got closer, I could see that the table was covered with platters of food: YummCo Yummy Pizza Pouches, Widdle Piggies, Super Cheezy Nachos, Slushers, and YummDogs. Most of them were eaten.

"Yolanda said her father tried to get in the way of her plan," I remembered. "She said she figured out a way to deal with him."

Mr. Yumm turned around. His hair was askew. His trademark suit was covered with smeared food. And his eyes were wide and glassy.

"Be smart, not dumb-dumb-dumb-co. And fill your day with YummCo," he chanted. Then he smiled, yellow Cheezy Nacho cheese spilling from his mouth.

Nina screamed.

Yolanda appeared in the doorway. "There they are!" she cried.

The YummCo workers rushed in behind her. We tried to put up a fight, but they managed to grab all of us with ease.

"Boys, I want you to take these children down to the lab and lock them up," Yolanda bellowed. "Eventually, they'll get hungry. Then we'll give them

the choice: starve, or eat some *delicious* new YummCo treats."

"Fortified with Yummconium," Danny whispered. Yolanda's green eyes glittered.

"You're not going to get away with this!" I yelled.

"Watch me," Yolanda said, smiling. As the YummCo workers dragged us away, I heard her say, "Daddy, can I interest you in some yum-yum-yummy dessert?"

CHAPTER TWELVE

K ari looked up as the lab door swung open. The guards entered with Mellie Gore and all her little friends.

"What are *you* doing here?" she asked.

The guards didn't answer; they opened the empty cages on the other side of the lab, the ones made for bigger animals, and shoved the children inside. The girl who wasn't Mellie Gore put her hands over her face and began to cry.

Ping!

Kari looked down at the new message on her YummPad.

"The Big Boss says that when these kids get hungry, we're supposed to . . . give them some of the new food," she said, blinking.

"What?" said Greg, his eyes going wide. "I definitely didn't sign up for this."

"You signed up for pretending to like my *mom*," one of the boys said from inside his cage. *He must be Roxanne Hurley's son,* Kari thought fleetingly.

"I was only pretending at first. And I had no idea *this* was why," Greg tried to explain. "Your mom is nice. Really nice."

"If you're such a nice guy, why don't you let us out?" one of the other boys asked.

"Because it's his *job*," Kari said. "When you're older and you all have jobs, you'll understand that when you're told to do something, you do it."

"Even when it's wrong?" said the third boy. "That seems pretty weak."

Kari's YummPad pinged again. "Okay, you all need to be quiet," she said. "The Big Boss just sent another message." She leaned over and nudged Greg and showed the YummPad to him.

"Is she serious?" Greg asked.

"When is she not?" said Kari. "I don't understand. She wants this done by *tomorrow*, worldwide?"

"She might come up with the 'huge' plans, but we're the ones left to make them happen," said Greg.

Kari sighed.

"I'll go talk to the Big Boss. You stay here and watch . . . everyone," Kari said, eyeing the children as she left, then closing the lab door behind her.

CHAPTER THIRTEEN

The more he understood the humans, the more he could understand why Brother was so angry. The one called Kari and the one called Greg were just as easily led as the others—not by a formula made in a lab, but by their own fear and weakness.

He tried to focus on Mellie and her friends, who were so brave. He wished he could hear what they were saying, but they were whispering. Were they planning something, too? He knew she couldn't understand him, but maybe she'd recognize his voice.

"Mellie!" Bert called. "I'm here! I'm here!"

CHAPTER FOURTEEN

Being put in a cage was pretty much the worst thing that had ever happened to me; now I knew how animals felt. Once the electronic doors were locked, I was sure we were done for.

That's when I yawned.

Uh-oh.

"What's up with you?" Danny whispered. He was in the cage next to me.

"What do you mean?" I said.

"You've been acting weird since the Harvest Festival. You're super tired, then you eat everything in sight, then you're hypersensitive to smells and sounds, then you're a hyper know-it-all," Danny said. "I know you, and I'm not stupid."

I leaned in so the others wouldn't hear me. "Okay, but don't freak out."

"We're locked in cages in the middle of a zombie attack, and we just heard that Yolanda wants to ship Yummconium worldwide. How much more freaked out could I get?" Danny asked. He had a point.

"Well, remember when Bert scratched me at the Harvest Festival?"

"At the end of your Best Pet performance. Yeah, I remember," Danny said, nodding.

"I think whatever happened to him is happening to me," I said.

His eyes widened. "But it seems . . . different from what's happened to everyone else in Lambert. You're not a zombie like them."

"Mellie's a *zombie?*" Nina shrieked.

"WHAT?" Carl yelled from the cage on the other side of Danny. Owen, who was in the cage on my right, pressed himself up against the side of his cage, closer to Nina.

"You kids need to be *quiet*," Greg called from his desk.

We all were, for about a minute.

"I'm not a zombie," I whispered. "See? I don't have glassy eyes. I'm not drooling, and I'm not violent. I just seem to get weak if I let myself go without eating for too long. And when I do eat, it feels *amazing*. It's more like the way Bert was. Or the way Bert is, wherever he is."

And then I heard it.

"Mellie! I'm here! I'm here!"

The voice sounded familiar, and yet . . . not. It was hard to move around the cage, but I managed to crane my neck to look around. I saw rabbits, mice, rats, a couple of small dogs, hamsters, guinea pigs, and some baby chicks. Then I saw the cats. One in particular, a gray striped cat, looked like a huge version of Bert; they were taking up almost their entire cage. I was so shocked by how big they were, I almost didn't see who was in the cage next to them.

"Bert? Is that . . . you?"

"It's me!" he said.

For a moment, I thought I might be dreaming. Because I could *understand him.*

"Bert, do you understand what I'm saying?" I asked.

"I've been able to understand you for a while," he said. *"Can you understand me?"*

"Whoa. And yes," I said.

"Who are you talking to?" Carl asked.

"To Bert," I said. "I think we understand each other now. It must be another side effect of the original Yummconium formula."

"Can you understand all the animals here, or just Bert?" Danny asked.

I concentrated and looked around the lab. It started as a murmur, but eventually, I started to pick up on other voices and other conversations. The mice were worried about who would be fed to the cats next. The guinea pigs wanted their water bottle refilled. The rats were playing a game to occupy themselves. The baby chicks were huddled together, scared.

"I think I understand them all," I said. "It's not necessarily a good thing."

"We need to stop Yolanda's plans," said Danny.

"But how?" asked Owen. "We're never going to get out of these cages."

"We're trapped here," said Nina. We all shivered. Then I yawned.

"Are you okay?" Danny asked.

All at once, it felt as if every ounce of energy left my body. I reached for my backpack.

"Yeah, I just need to eat something. But don't worry; I brought a snack."

I'd been in such a hurry on my way out of the house, I hadn't zipped the backpack all the way shut. It was a good thing, too, because I didn't have a lot of strength to open it. But when I reached inside, I didn't feel a granola bar. I felt something furry.

"What the—?" I said. My backpack dropped to the cage floor. A tiny, familiar head popped out.

"Zoomer!" Carl cried. He opened his suit jacket and looked inside. "In all the craziness, I didn't even realize you'd gotten loose."

"I didn't even realize you'd brought him," Danny said.

"He likes hanging out in my pocket," Carl explained.

"He also likes eating other people's granola bars," I said, feeling around in my backpack. "And the wrappers, too."

I turned my backpack over and gave it a shake. Only my phone fell out; it tumbled through the cage bars and skittered across the floor. Greg swiveled around in his chair.

"What's going on here?" he said.

Carl cleared his throat. "Uh, nothing, sir."

"Well, let's keep it that way. The quieter you are, the better off you'll be," Greg said. Then he went back to work.

We all looked at one another. Nina reached out of her cage and grabbed my phone. She held it up and smiled.

"We can call Mrs. Witt!" she whispered. I told her the number, and she started dialing.

"What's happening?" Owen asked.

After a few seconds of listening, Nina frowned. "No reception," she said. "Now what do we do?"

"I'm feeling . . . really . . . weak," I managed. I could barely form the words; my brain had gone fuzzy again.

"Check your pockets," Danny said to the others. "One of us must have some kind of snack."

Everyone patted themselves down, but no snacks emerged. I no longer had the strength to sit up, so I curled up on the floor of my cage and closed my eyes.

"What now?" Carl asked.

"Uh, Greg?" Danny said. "Do you have something my friend could eat?"

"I'm supposed to give you some of our new food when you're hungry," I heard Greg reply. "Those are my orders from the Big Boss."

"She's really sick, Greg. I thought you were a *nice guy*," Danny said.

The next thing I knew, something was dangling in my face. I opened one eye. It was a bag of Witt Fizzles, and the hand dangling it belonged to Greg.

"Where did you get those?" Carl asked.

"They've been in my desk. I think they belonged to the guy who worked here before me," Greg explained.

"Mr. Witt," Nina whispered.

"Give them to me," I heard Danny say. "I'll feed them to her. And Greg?"

"Yeah, buddy?"

"Thanks."

Over the next few minutes, Danny gave me one Witt Fizzle after another. After about the tenth one,

I could sit up on my own. Eventually, my brain went back to its buzzy self, but only after I'd emptied the whole bag.

"Whoa," said Owen. "And I thought *I* ate a lot of candy."

"Okay, now we need to figure out how to get out of here," I said. I looked all around the lab.

"I already have a plan," Bert said.

I looked at him. "Are you sure?"

"What's he saying?" Owen asked.

"He says he has a plan," I explained.

"We're going to trust a *cat* to rescue us?" Carl asked. "A *zombie* cat?"

"How many times do we have to tell you—he's *not* a zombie," Danny said.

I was still looking at Bert.

"Just act worried," he said.

"That won't be hard," I replied.

CHAPTER FIFTEEN

*F*inally, the moment had come. It was time to set the next phase of his plan into motion. He was ready.

He rolled onto his back and started moaning.

The one named Greg hurried over. "What's going on?" he asked.

"It's Bert . . . I mean, Y-91," Mellie cried. "I think there's something wrong with him."

"First you, now the cat?" Greg said, scratching his head.

Bert rolled his eyes. He twitched and drooled.

"Do something!" one of the other children shouted. Greg ran back to his desk and pressed a series of buttons. The cage opened.

"Okay, Y-91, let's take a look at you," Greg said, putting on thick gloves.

"Mrooooooooow, mrooooooooow," Bert moaned, his eyes shut tight as he was placed on the examining table.

"You really do seem to be in pain," Greg said, leaning down to get a closer look.

ROWR!

All at once, Bert growled and jumped up, knocking Greg right off his feet. Then he scrambled over to the YummPad and started pushing at it with his paws.

"What are you doing?" Mellie shouted.

"I've been watching them all this time. I know all their secrets," he said. With a beep and a whoosh, all the cage doors opened.

The one named Greg looked around as everyone, human and animal, emerged from their cages. His eyes grew wide. Then he quickly punched in a code, ran out the lab door, and punched the code in again from the other side, shutting it behind him.

CHAPTER SIXTEEN

I did my best to ignore all the chaos as I opened all of the refrigerators.

"What are you looking for, Mellie?" Danny asked.

"There has to be an antidote here somewhere," I said.

We all put on gloves, just to be safe, and then everyone started searching with me.

"They sure were doing a lot of experiments," Nina noted. "These poor animals."

"So much for YummCo's cruelty-free pledge," said Carl.

"Hey, check this out," Owen said. He pulled out
a rack of stoppered vials of green liquid. They were all
marked YC COUNTERAGENT.

"Bingo," I said. Owen and Nina helped me load
the vials into my backpack.

"But we're still all trapped in here," Danny
reminded us.

"No problem," I said. "When I saw how Bert
memorized the code to open the cages, I made sure to
watch Greg when he was opening the lab door."

I punched in the code.

BEEEP. Whoosh.

"As long as we don't hit the code again, it should stay open," I explained.

"Impressive," Carl said.

"We're free!" Nina cried, clapping her hands. "Let's go!"

CHAPTER SEVENTEEN

H e did his best to help all of the other animals out of their cages.

"So, your plan worked," Brother said. He was standing just outside his cage, licking a beefy paw.

"I said I would save everyone," Bert said. "I keep my promises."

"Some of these animals have never seen the outside of a cage," Brother said. "They won't know how to survive."

"They'll learn," Bert said.

"They don't stand a chance. Not in a world where

humans rule, where they're still out to harm us, capture us, use us for their terrible, selfish plans. We're all still in a cage now. It's just . . . bigger."

"They're not all like that. Mellie and her friends aren't like that," Bert tried to explain.

"You've grown too trusting of the humans. Let them destroy each other. Then we will truly be free," Brother said.

"Never."

"It's clear the first version of the humans' formula was a failure. It was supposed to make you stronger," Brother said. "Instead, you've grown . . . soft. Or perhaps you've always been that way. Our mother should have drowned you in the river when she had the chance, Brother."

"My name is *Bert*. And my promise to save everyone includes the humans, too. Even if I have to save them from themselves," he said. And then he rushed off to join his friends.

CHAPTER EIGHTEEN

I think we might actually have a signal," Nina said, holding up our phone as we walked down a long corridor.

"Call Mrs. Witt," I said.

She picked up right away. Nina put her on speaker phone.

"Thank goodness," Mrs. Witt said. "I was really starting to worry. Are you all okay?"

"We're fine," I said. I gave the blueprint of the factory to Danny so he could continue navigating.

"We found Bert, and the antidote, but it looks like Yummconium is about to be added to even more food and shipped all over the world. Now what do we do?"

"We'll need to put the antidote in something that everyone exposed to Yummconium can ingest," Mrs. Witt said. "Drinking water is an obvious choice, so maybe the reservoir? Everyone is going to get thirsty at some point."

"Right," I said. But "at some point" seemed pretty far off. Could we afford to wait that long? And how could we get the zombies of Lambert to drink plain water when they were hypnotized to consume nothing but YummCo products?

"Mellie, you're going to want to see this," Danny said. I followed him up a metal staircase and through a door that said FILLING AND PACKING.

We all stood on a catwalk, looking down on a series of enormous vats and machines.

"What's in the vats?" I asked.

"According to the packaging, it looks like it's called *Yummystuff*," Carl said. "Some kind of marshmallow crème that you can put on ice cream or spread on a sandwich."

"My teeth hurt just thinking about it," said Nina.

"Really? I think it sounds *amazing*," said Owen.

I turned back to the phone. "What about marsh-mallow crème?" I asked Mrs. Witt. "We're seeing a big vat of it here. Will that work?"

"If you can get everyone to eat it, sure," she said.

"We'll figure out a way," I said.

"I know you will," she said. "Keep me posted."

I hung up the phone and gave it back to Nina. "Okay," I said to everyone. "Danny and I are going to put the antidote in the vat and get all of the containers filled and packed. Can the rest of you figure out how to get the boxes onto one of the trucks in the loading bay?"

"My dad lets me drive his car sometimes," Carl said. "But only in the Super YummCo parking lot when there's no one else around."

"Good enough," I said.

"But then what?" Danny asked.

"We deliver the antidote to everyone here in Lambert, and if we can't stop Yummconium from shipping worldwide, then we figure out a way to get the antidote to everyone else," I explained.

"That . . . sounds impossible," said Owen.

I remembered the Marie Curie poster back in my bedroom, her wise words burned into my brain.

"'I was taught that the way of progress was neither swift nor easy,'" I said. "Let's go."

CHAPTER NINETEEN

I can't believe you let those kids escape. And now all the animals are free, including Y-91 *and* Y-92?" Kari said, storming down the hallway.

"They're out of their cages, but they're still locked in the lab," Greg explained, trailing behind her. "I figured that would keep them safe. I wasn't about to turn a bunch of kids into zombies."

Kari whirled around. "So you disobeyed the Big Boss's orders?"

"It was the right thing to do. What the Big Boss is doing is wrong. You know it's true," Greg said. "Or are you just a zombie, like everyone else?"

"Yummconium is a game-changing advancement. We're helping consumers to find their best selves," Kari reminded him. But Greg grabbed her YummPad. He turned it around and shoved it in her face so she could see the live feed.

A toddler, no more than two or three, had knocked over an elderly couple and was climbing over them to get to the last jar of Yummy Nutty Peanut Butter. Several people, including two police officers, were fighting out front over a case of Diet Root Beer YummPop. Even the YummCo workers in the store had stopped doing their jobs; instead, they were yanking merchandise from people in the checkout line, tearing open the boxes and containers, and feasting.

"Do they look like their best selves?" Greg shouted. "These 'consumers' are our friends, our neighbors, people we love. Look what we've turned them into. LOOK!"

"I am looking," Kari said quietly. But she didn't seem to be able to fix her eyes on the screen.

"Well, then, you're not seeing what I'm seeing," Greg said, walking ahead of her.

"This is an important job. I'm supposed to make my parents proud," Kari shouted after him. "I'm up for a *promotion!* Where are you going?"

"To put a stop to all of this," Greg said, climbing the stairs to the filling and packing area.

"You're going to ruin everything!" Kari yelled.

"I certainly hope so!" Greg said cheerfully. He opened the door.

CHAPTER TWENTY

U h-oh," Danny said. He pointed up to the catwalk. Greg and Kari had just walked through the
door. Greg looked surprised, and Kari looked . . . not
happy.

"What is going on here?" she shouted, descending
the metal staircase. "How did these children escape?"

"We're saving Lambert. And hopefully the world,"
I said, pouring all of the antidote vials into the vat. I
could have taken some of it then, but I knew we all
needed my buzzy super-brain. And I have to admit, I
wanted to hang on to it as long as I could.

Kari looked at Greg. "You let these children have the antidote?" But Greg just shrugged. When she turned back around, he gave us all the thumbs-up.

"There's only two of you, and five of us," Danny said.

"Make that six," said Greg.

"So you can either help us or get out of the way," I said.

"I'm calling security," she said, pulling out her phone.

"The security guards are mesmerized like everyone else," Danny said. "They'll only answer to Yolanda. So you really don't have a choice here."

"Open the doors to the loading dock!" I called down to Carl. "I'm going to start the filling and packing machines!"

Carl gave me a little salute, then hit the button to open the loading dock doors. "Wait," Danny said as the doors slowly lifted. "Do you hear that?"

Sadly, I did.

CHAPTER TWENTY-ONE

Y ummCo brings the fun-co!
The fun has just begun-co!
Be smart, not dumb-dumb-dumb-co!
And fill your day with YummCo!

The jingle played on a loop programmed on the Big Boss's YummPad. She regarded the horde before her; she'd summoned everyone in Lambert, including all the YummCo workers, to the loading dock, where they awaited her instructions.

Yolanda Yumm had never felt such power. She'd been waiting for this moment for a long time. She smoothed her perfect hair. Then she smiled her perfect smile and spoke into her bullhorn.

"Greetings, my people!" she said, her voice echoing across the dock. "The fun has just begun-co!"

"Hungry," moaned someone in the crowd.

"Need . . . buy . . . more!" moaned another.

"Fill our day with YummCo!" cried a third.

"You'll get everything you want and more. I promise," she said. "But first, I need you to help me get my trucks loaded up and on the road to where my cargo ships and planes are waiting. It's time we increased the power of my army and introduced Yummconium to the rest of the world—then, everything and everyone will be under my control!"

The horde cheered—as much as zombies could cheer. Mostly they shuffled their feet and lolled their heads.

Kari's voice crackled over Yolanda's headset.

"Boss, we have a problem."

"What is it?" the Big Boss said sharply.

"Mellie Gore and her friends," Kari said. "They're

here, in the filling and packing area. And they have the antidote."

Yolanda stomped her foot. "I thought we'd taken care of those brats," she said.

"For the record, it's Greg's fault," Kari said.

Mellie Gore appeared in the loading dock doorway.

"We've added the antidote to the Yummystuff. It's all over, Yolanda," she announced.

"It's over when *I* say it's over. Nothing is going to stop my plan now, especially not a group of pathetic *children*. And not when I have an entire town in my power," Yolanda said. She used her YummPad to turn up the volume of the jingle. "People of Lambert, seize those kids!"

CHAPTER TWENTY-TWO

The horde of Lambert townspeople advanced toward us. Not the best time for my hunger pangs to start again. I sank to the floor.

"Mellie!" Danny cried. But I was too weak to respond.

"Yolanda sicced the whole town on us! What do we do now?" Owen asked.

"Maybe we need to sic something on *her*," Carl asked. He managed to pull Zoomer out of his suit pocket and lifted him up so he got a good look at Yolanda. Then he took out his special whistle and blew it in a certain rhythm. I could hear it, but only barely.

In a flash, Zoomer jumped out of Carl's hands and scampered across the concrete, all the way to Yolanda.

"What the—" she said, looking down. Her green eyes met Zoomer's dark, beady ones.

"AAAAAH!" Yolanda screamed. When Zoomer jumped up on her dress and started climbing, Yolanda dropped her YummPad. It clattered to the ground and the YummCo jingle stopped playing. The townspeople stopped, too.

"Whew! That was close," Nina said.

Danny exhaled. "Now one of us just needs to get back in there to start the filling and packing machines." He looked around. "Bert?"

Mroooooow.

I lifted my head. Bert was at the foot of the Yummystuff vat. The big striped gray cat, the one that was in the cage next to him in the lab, was advancing toward him. Both of them had puffed-up fur, and they were growling.

I summoned all the strength I had left to call to him.

"BERT!"

CHAPTER TWENTY-THREE

He thought he heard a voice call to him, but he was in no position to respond.

"You're no match for me," Brother growled, his fangs dripping with drool.

"You might be bigger than me now," Bert said. "But you're still small inside."

"I'll show you how small I am. Come closer, Brother." He flicked out all the claws on one paw. "Everything has led up to this moment."

"It would seem so," said Bert.

"I can't let you save the humans," Brother said. "Not after everything they've done to both of us. To our family."

"Well," said Bert. "I can't let you stop me."

They both leaped at each other, shrieking and rolling around on the floor. Bert broke free and ran up the stairs, Brother nipping at his heels. Finally, Brother caught up to him, grabbing Bert by the scruff of his neck and slamming him into the railing. Bert stopped moving.

"That was almost too easy," Brother said. He leaned in to sniff the body, to make sure it was dead. But just as his nose touched fur, Bert jumped up, sinking his teeth into his foe's ear.

"MROOOOOOOOW!" Brother cried. Bert ran past him, across the catwalk, toward the controls that start the filling process. Brother was at his heels again, panting.

"It's over," Bert said.

"It is," said Brother. "For you."

Brother lunged at him, but at the last moment, Bert leaped to the side. The other cat sailed over the edge, right into the vat of Yummystuff.

"Brother!" Bert cried. He leaned over, extending a paw. "Grab on to me!"

"You're a fool to think you can save everyone," Brother growled, sinking into the sticky goo. "And you're a fool to trust humans. They ruin . . . everything."

"Bert!" a voice called.

He turned. Below, he saw Mellie, lying on the floor. Something was very wrong.

"Mellie!" he called back.

"Remember," she said weakly, her eyes fighting to stay open. "Our training."

Bert looked back at the vat, where his brother was sinking out of sight. He blinked. He knew what he had to do.

As they'd trained together for the Best Pet Contest, Bert got up on his hind legs. But instead of touching his nose to a YummCo sticker, he hit the button to start the filling and packing process. The machines sputtered and roared to life.

Or, at least, they started to. And then they stopped. The vat began to shudder.

"What's wrong?" Danny shouted. "It sounds like the vat's overloaded."

"Maybe something's stuck in it," Nina said.

Or *someone,* Bert thought.

A hissing sound grew louder and louder as pressure built up in the shuddering vat. The ground started shaking.

"This can't be good," said Carl.

CHAPTER TWENTY-FOUR

*B*OOM!

When the vat finally exploded, everyone else was knocked to the floor around me. None of us were hurt, but we couldn't get far; the sticky green Yummystuff had splattered everywhere, all over everyone and everything. I'd never seen such a mess.

That was the bad news. The good news was that when it splattered all over everyone, people in the horde started eating it. Within an hour, everyone was back to normal. Well, aside from being covered with sticky green goo.

I was still too weak to stand, so I forced myself to eat handfuls of the Yummystuff, too, though I knew it wouldn't cure me like the others. Filling my empty stomach did give me a little bit of strength, even if the Yummystuff tasted almost painfully sweet. I climbed over Yolanda and grabbed her bullhorn.

"Mom? Dad? It's Mellie," I called. "Are you out there?"

For the first minute, I didn't hear anything. Then, from far away, I heard a noise. Shouting. As it grew closer, I recognized their voices.

"Oh, honey!" my mother said as she and Dad wrapped me in a sticky embrace.

"I don't know what came over us," my father said.

"I do," I said. "I'll explain when we get home."

And then I remembered.

"Wait . . . where's Bert?"

I ran back into the factory.

"Don't go in there, Mellie!" my dad called. "It's dangerous!"

But I didn't care. All I cared about was Bert. He'd saved me. He'd saved all of us. Now I needed to save him.

Globs and piles of Yummystuff and pieces of broken, twisted equipment littered the concrete floor of the filling and packing area.

"Bert?" I called. "Bert?"

The more I said his name, the more tears began to fall.

"Mrrrrr-rrrr?"

I stopped. I tried to filter out all the other noise.

"Bert?" I said again.

"Rrrr . . . mmmm . . . hmmmmmrrr!"

"Keep making noise, Bert!" I cried. "I hear you!"

"Hrrrr! Crrrrr . . . mmrrrrrrm."

I followed the faint sound of his voice to a small vat that had gotten filled with Yummy-stuff. I plunged both my arms in, elbow-deep, and felt around until I touched something solid.

"Mellie!" Danny called, appearing at my side.

Carl, Owen, and Nina joined us. "What's going on?" said Carl.

"Help me!" I cried. "It's Bert!"

Together, we pulled him out. Bert was completely covered in Yummystuff, to the point where we had to pull it away from his nose and mouth and eyes and ears. He took a few deep breaths, and then he managed to speak.

"Is everyone okay?" he asked.

"Everyone is fine," I informed him.

"You saved us all," said Carl.

Bert craned his neck to look around. *"I hope so."*

The sound of sirens filled the air. A fire truck pulled up from Bridgedale, the next town over, along with several ambulances and two police cars. And then a big black car. While the police officers and firefighters and EMTs assessed the crowd, two women in dark suits got out of the black car. They made a beeline for Yolanda.

"Yolanda Yumm?" one of the women said. "I'm FDA Agent Rita Denise, and this is FBI Agent Niki Michalak. You're coming with us."

Yolanda managed to stand. She tried to smooth her hair, which was matted down with sticky green

Yummystuff, but Agent Denise was quick to pull her hands behind her back and cuff her.

"Whatever for?" Yolanda asked. "I'm just another victim here. Someone just sabotaged my father's factory, and I suspect they poisoned a batch of YummCo food that was served to the townspeople yesterday. I'm certain it was my father's lab assistants, Kari Ray and Greg Devany. You'll find Kari's name on every authorization involved in this incident. And I've never trusted Greg."

"That's interesting," said Agent Denise. "Since Greg Devany is actually Greg Scott, one of our agents. In fact, he's my partner."

"*What?*" Yolanda shrieked.

"What?" Danny said. Greg emerged from the loading bay with Kari. He shook the other agents' hands.

"Agent Scott," Agent Denise said. "We came as soon as you called."

"Backup is on its way," added Agent Michalak.

"Great. Just about everything we'll need is recorded here," Agent Scott said, handing his partner his phone.

Kari gasped. "You've been recording me all this time? So *that's* why you always made me explain everything to you," she said.

"I'm a lot smarter than I look," Agent Scott said, grinning. He looked at the other agents and nodded. "Let's get Ms. Ray and Ms. Yumm into custody ASAP. We have a *lot* to talk about."

As Agents Denise and Michalak handcuffed Kari and Yolanda and read them their rights, Agent Scott approached us.

"How's your cat?" he asked as I cradled a very sticky Bert.

"He's okay, I think," I said.

"I'll put in a call to the vet in Bridgedale," he said. "YummCo Animal Pals has been closed, pending our investigation."

"So . . . you're an agent?" Danny asked.

"Yeah, my office received a tip from a whistle-blower about six months ago, but he died before we could follow up," Agent Scott said.

"Mr. Witt," I said.

Agent Scott nodded. "So I had to go undercover at YummCo for a while, until we had all the evidence

we needed. I'm sorry I couldn't tell you kids until now, but I was sworn to secrecy."

"You spied on us for YummCo, but all the while you were investigating them? So you were, like, a *double agent*." Danny said. "Cool."

"Tell your mom I'll give her a call," Agent Scott said. "She deserves an explanation from me."

"I'll put in a good word for you," Danny said.

Agent Scott raised his eyebrows. "I'd appreciate it."

As Yolanda was being shoved in the back of the agents' car, she spotted me and Bert.

"It's all that cat's fault!" she shouted.

"Yes," I murmured, scratching Bert under his sticky chin. "I suppose it is."

CHAPTER TWENTY-FIVE

*L*ater that night, after he'd been tended to by the gentle hands of the veterinarian in Bridgedale and Mellie had taken him home, Bert was exhausted. But he couldn't sleep. Mellie let him out her bedroom window that night and he made his way to the cemetery.

When the vat exploded, he was thrown quite a distance. The whole thing seemed to happen in slow motion. Before he landed and the Yummystuff covered him, he glimpsed a familiar shape propelled from the vat, soaring across the sky. Now Bert headed in that same direction. He slipped through the black metal bars of the fence, then wound his way through the rows of stones, sniffing the air as he went.

But Brother was nowhere to be found. Bert perched on one of the stones and looked out onto YummCo. It had been his prison and the cause of his family's destruction. But it was there that he'd met Mellie, who'd given him his true home. Now it was over. What would his life be like without the need for revenge?

The sun would be rising soon, and he still needed to eat, and then he needed to get back to Mellie. He padded across the grass, the first frost of the season cool on his paws.

He passed the largest, tallest stone in the wide yard, the one with the green metal man on top. It towered over him, though now he could read the words etched into the stone: NATHANIEL LAMBERT. He'd ask Mellie what those words meant when he got home. Around the stone was an arrangement of five perfectly rounded shrubs.

But there were only four now. Four living shrubs, anyway. The fifth was crushed, its leafy branches

flattened in a circle, as if something had landed on it with extreme force, or from an extreme height. Or both.

He crept closer and sniffed at the trail of broken bits of branch and foliage and familiar green goo, which led off through the cemetery, in the direction of town . . . or perhaps the woods they called home so long ago? He listened. He sniffed again. He looked around. Though all his senses told him he was alone here, Bert spoke aloud anyway.

"You were wrong, Brother," he said. "I did keep my promise."

CHAPTER TWENTY-SIX

It was a lovely, crisp, clear fall morning in Hardfield, a few towns over from Lambert. One would have found it difficult not to enjoy the beauty of the day—unless one was locked inside the US penitentiary located there.

Though she was just visiting, Kari definitely wasn't thrilled about being there; after all, she would have been sent to prison herself if it weren't for the deal she'd struck with the feds. She shouldn't even be here, given that deal. But she'd been summoned.

She sat in the waiting area and tried not to make eye contact with any of the inmates and their families. She tried not to think about what her parents would think of her being there. She hadn't heard from them since they found out what happened at YummCo and her role in it all, so maybe what they thought shouldn't matter as much anymore. All she wanted was to make them proud, and instead, she'd lost herself completely. She'd become an outcast, and very nearly a criminal.

At exactly eleven o'clock, the inmate was brought in by two guards. Her hair was in a ponytail and she wore no makeup; still, she managed to look more elegant than anyone else in the room. How did she do it?

"Hello, Kari," Yolanda said, her eyes cold.

"Hello, Yolanda," Kari said. "You look . . . well."

Yolanda scoffed. "You must need glasses," she said.

"It's the first time I haven't seen you in green and brown," Kari said. "Not even at the trial. The gray uniform . . . suits you."

"You're too kind," Yolanda said. "Actually, since

you testified against me in exchange for immunity, you're not kind *at all*."

"What did you expect me to do?" Kari whispered. "Go to jail? My parents would kill me."

"Well." Yolanda exhaled and looked at the guards, then back at Kari. "I need you to do me a favor."

"Yolanda."

"Don't worry, it's nothing illegal," she said, smiling. "I just need you to deliver a letter for me. You can get it from my attorney. I would have given it to you directly today, but then the guards would have to read it first."

"You want me to deliver a letter?" Kari said.

"Yes. It's the least you can do for me, under the circumstances," Yolanda said. "And don't read it. It's personal business."

"I guess I can do that," Kari said. "You know, I'm sorry it turned out this way. I looked up to you; you were like my mentor, until, you know, you decided to turn the entire world into zombies. Including your own father."

Yolanda shrugged. "He's fully recovered from the Yummconium, like all the others," she said.

"Though I hear he has bigger problems now. He and his lawyers."

Kari looked at her watch. "I should really get going."

"You should. There's a lot of work to be done," said Yolanda. Then she called for the guards.

"Goodbye," Kari said as the guards took Yolanda away.

"Come visit again soon," she said.

"I don't think I will," Kari said. "No offense."

"None taken," Yolanda said, smiling. "I don't plan to be in here very long, anyway."

CHAPTER TWENTY-SEVEN

So much happened in the months that followed, between the arrests and the investigation and the trial, the recovery of everyone in Lambert, the cleanup of the town itself, and all the crazy media attention. When my birthday rolled around, it seemed as good a time as any to have a party. It felt good to do something even halfway normal.

We kept it small; other than me and my parents and the twins, we invited Danny, Carl, Nina, Owen, their parents, their pets, and Mrs. Witt. She brought a fresh batch of Witt Fizzles, and we all helped ourselves to at least one.

"I'm really glad you're making candy again," Danny said. "And I'm not just saying that because of the free samples."

"I'm thinking of reopening Witts Confectionery, where YummCo Animal Pals used to be. Just a little storefront, like the one Walter and I first had. Though it won't be the same without him," Mrs. Witt said. "I'd trade all the money in the world to bring him back. Though if I can do my part to rid this town of any trace of YummCo, that's something."

We were all quiet then. The Witt Fizzle I was eating was perfectly sweet and sour on my tongue. It seemed fitting, how YummCo bought Witts Confectionery and now Mrs. Witt was about to buy it back. And the Yumms needed every penny they could get, with all the lawsuits from everyone who ate the Yummconium-tainted food at the Harvest Festival. The people of Lambert had a new hunger: for justice, by way of compensation.

"Well," Mrs. Witt said, breaking the silence. She patted Danny's leg. "It's nice to have a chance to see you again before your move."

It was sad but true; Danny and his mom were

moving to Hardfield, where Ms. Hurley had found a new job. When the factory and the grocery store and everything else owned by YummCo closed so fast, just about everyone in town was out of a job. But Danny was busier than ever, working on a new movie for his Hurlvision channel. Since the incident at YummCo, his films had really taken off.

"I'll be just a bus ride away," Danny reminded her. He gestured to my new smartphone, a birthday gift from my parents. "Or a phone call."

"School won't be the same without you," I said.

He nudged me. "We'll always be the Weirdo Twins," he said. I nudged him back.

"Who wants more pizza?" my dad asked, bringing out a fresh pie with my favorite toppings, bacon and broccoli, which he'd arranged in the shape of an *M* for Mellie. He was still cooking, but he and my mom had stopped filming for their vlog. Instead, Mom was going back to her journalism roots and helping me put together my exposé of YummCo. I was interested in getting the truth out there after Yolanda had told so many lies, and my mom had the idea to turn it into a podcast, which she wanted to call *The*

ZomBert Chronicles. I had to admit, it had a certain ring to it.

"Pizza for me!" Emmett said, holding out his plate. "Make sure mine has broccoli!"

"Me, too!" said Ezra.

"Me, three!" I said. I checked the time on my phone. I'd gotten used to making sure I ate regularly before I got too weak.

"I brought a little something else for you," Mrs. Witt whispered to me. She opened her purse just wide enough for me to get a peek at the little stoppered vial.

"You finally figured out an antidote for me and Bert?" I said.

"Walter always said I was just as good a chemist as he was," she said, laughing. "Maybe even better. There was a bit of trial and error, coming up with a special counteragent to treat the original formula for Yummconium, but I love a challenge."

I looked at the stairs.

"What's the matter?" Mrs. Witt asked, frowning. "Don't tell me you're having second thoughts."

"No." I knew taking the antidote was the right

thing to do. As much as I liked so many of the powers the Yummconium gave me, the hunger really was
overwhelming. And more than anything, I just didn't
feel like myself. It was more satisfying to learn all the
answers naturally on my own, not have them come
to me in a weird buzzy rush. It seemed too much like
cheating.

But it wasn't just about me.

"Tell my parents about the antidote. I'm sure
they'll be thrilled," I said. "I'll be right back."

CHAPTER TWENTY-EIGHT

H e was curled up on Mellie's bed; he wasn't much for parties. And he needed all the sleep he could get before a night of hunting.

"Hi," Bert heard her say.

He opened one eye. *"Hi, yourself,"* he said.

"It looks like your fur is starting to grow in again," Mellie noted.

"It's a good thing. The weather's getting colder."

The vet in Bridgedale had had to shave him, he'd been so covered with the sticky Yummystuff. But he was no stranger to losing things. And gaining them back.

"So . . . Mrs. Witt is downstairs," she said quietly. "With the antidote."

"We knew this day would come," he said.

"I'm going to miss you," Mellie said.

"I'm not going anywhere."

"Well, yes and no," said Mellie. "I mean, you'll still be here. But we won't be able to understand each other. Not like this."

He looked at her. *"We'll always have an understanding."*

"She can give you the antidote, too," Mellie reminded him. "I know you said you didn't want it, but I just thought I'd see if you'd changed your mind."

His mind was still racing, searching, connecting, as it had been for some time. There were so many things for him to learn, and to know.

"I'm sure," he said. *"You're still growing into who you are. But I am who I am now. I can't go back."* And he knew he needed all his strength and power. As long as Brother was still out there, Bert would keep searching.

"Okay," she said. She reached out a hand and touched the tag that dangled from his new collar. It said BERT, along with her new phone number. She'd given him his name, and his home, and though she'd never be his owner—no one would—she'd become something even more precious: his friend.

Mellie opened her bedroom window a crack so he could go out hunting when he was ready.

"I'll see you in the morning," she said.

"You will," he said. He blinked at her, then closed his eyes. There was still time to take just one more nap.

CHAPTER TWENTY-NINE

I was feeling great after Mrs. Witt gave me the antidote. It was weird to realize how not like myself I'd felt before. Now my thoughts came to me at a regular speed, and I didn't feel or hear or see every little thing. And I didn't feel like I would faint if I didn't inhale the entire two-tier chocolate caramel birthday cake my dad made. As my friends and family sang "Happy Birthday to You," I realized things were actually starting to seem normal again. I didn't even make a wish as I blew out the candles; I had every-thing I needed, right here.

And then the doorbell rang.

My parents answered the door. I couldn't imagine who it was because everyone we'd invited was already there. Just as I was telling Carl about the podcast idea, I saw her in the doorway. Kari.

"What are *you* doing here?" I asked. "Can't you see we're having a party?"

"And you're *definitely* not invited," Danny added over my shoulder.

"I didn't realize," she said. She looked at my mom and dad. "I just need to talk to Mellie for a minute. Then I'll go."

I rolled my eyes. "Fine," I said.

"Are you sure?" Mom asked me.

"It's okay to say no, kiddo," my dad said. "You don't have to do anything that makes you uncomfortable."

"It's fine, whatever," I said. I looked at Kari. "Let's go outside."

"Your parents seem nice," she said.

"They are," I said, folding my arms. "I really don't

want to make small talk; I want to get back to the party. So why are you here?"

Kari sighed. "Okay," she said.

She reached into the bag she was carrying and pulled out an envelope.

"This is from Yolanda," she said, handing it to me.

"Are you kidding?" I said. "Why would she think I would want something from her?"

"I have no idea. I'm just the messenger. She told me to deliver it to you, that's all."

Kari backed off my porch and down the steps.

"You can do whatever you want with it, I guess. Throw it away if you want," she said.

"Maybe I will."

"Okay. Goodbye, then. And sorry, for everything, by the way," she said. "Your parents really do seem very nice."

I looked down at the envelope. By the time I looked up again, she was gone.

I really, really wanted to throw it away. But as always, curiosity got the best of me.

I'll just read it quickly, and then I'll throw it away, I told myself. I tore it open and unfolded the letter, which turned out to be shorter than I expected.

Dear Emmeline,

I'm writing this to you from prison, where I assume you and everyone else think I should be.

I thought I should let you know that you are also at fault. You freed all of the lab animals from their cages, animals that were subjects of other experiments I was conducting. I haven't told anyone of these missing creatures, as I did not want to inspire further panic. But they are dangerous, and they must be retrieved. I hope you might be willing to take on this responsibility; I'll be happy to provide you with whatever materials you might need, as I am able from here.

Please let me know your response as soon as you can. You know where to find me.

Yours,
Yolanda Yumm

I folded the letter carefully and placed it back in its envelope. Then I walked back in the house.

Danny was filming as Nina was moving the paws of her cat, Felicity, in time to the pop song playing on Nina's phone. Owen was telling my mom how he got his bird, Mudge, to talk. Carl and the twins were looking at his rats while my dad laid out fresh slices of cake.

"Ready to eat, Mellie-Mel?" he asked me, holding out a plate.

"In a minute," I said.

I opened my bedroom door and turned on the light.

"Sorry to wake you up again," I said. "But it looks like we have more work to do."

Slowly, Bert opened one yellow eye.

ACKNOWLEDGMENTS

Thank you so much for coming along on this journey with me and Mellie and Bert. I hope you've enjoyed reading these books as much as I've enjoyed writing them. I've had a lot of help along the way, and I'm glad to have this opportunity to offer some words of gratitude.

Barry Goldblatt first suggested I write a story about a zombie cat. My editor, Sarah Ketchersid, took a chance on one very (very!) rough draft and two synopses and improved each story immeasurably with her wisdom and good humor. The brilliant and talented Ryan Andrews brought these characters and the town of Lambert to life. The team at Candlewick Press made these books look amazing and expertly ushered them into the world. My trusted readers, Anika Denise, Jamie Michalak, and Betsy Devany Macleod, offered me invaluable suggestions (and may have ended up as characters in these pages). Gale Pryor lent me her expertise on clicker training, a system originally developed by her mother, Karen.

My hometown of Stratford, Connecticut, inspired the setting of Lambert, and my childhood friends (most of whom are still my friends to this day) inspired Danny and the gang in the books. I'm so grateful my friends and I found one another and that we still always find time to reminisce and revel in our weirdness. For my young readers, I hope you also find friends who encourage you and love you for who you are—and who would follow you into zombie battle.

Of course, I am thankful for the love and support and patience of my husband, Scott, and our child, Camden. And last but not least, I offer gratitude and belly rubs to all the cats who've been my companions over the years—most recently Pearl and Sugar, who sadly did not live to see the end of this series, and Lulu and Ella, who have just joined our family and already inspire me with their mysterious ways.

KARA LaREAU is the author of many books for young readers, including *Rise of ZomBert* and *Return of ZomBert*, as well as the Theodor Seuss Geisel Honor Book *The Infamous Ratsos* and its sequels. She is also the author of the Unintentional Adventures of the Bland Sisters series of middle-grade novels. Kara LaReau lives in Providence, Rhode Island, with her family and their two cats.

RYAN ANDREWS is a comics artist and illustrator. He is the illustrator of *Rise of ZomBert* and *Return of ZomBert* by Kara LaReau and *The Dollar Kids* by Jennifer Richard Jacobson and the author-illustrator of the graphic novel *This Was Our Pact*. Two of his web comics have been nominated for Will Eisner Comic Industry Awards. Ryan Andrews lives in Fukuoka, Japan.